GOd, GOd, What DO YOU See?

Fearfully and Wonderfully Made

BJ FOSter

WestBow Press books may be ordered through booksellers or by contacting:

WestBow Press
A Division of Thomas Nelson & Zondervan
1663 Liberty Drive
Bloomington, IN 47403
www.westbowpress.com
844-714-3454

ISBN: 978-1-6642-4860-1 (sc)
ISBN: 978-1-6642-4862-5 (hc)
ISBN: 978-1-6642-4861-8 (e)

Library of Congress Control Number: 2021922313

Print information available on the last page.

WestBow Press rev. date: 11/24/2021

WESTBOW
PRESS®
A DIVISION OF THOMAS NELSON
& ZONDERVAN

Dear Mom and Dad,

Fitting in is every child's desire. At six years old, when a grade school friend asked, 'Whoa, who hit you in the eye?" I felt *different* for the first time. My unique birthmark, which up until now, *proudly* circled my left eye, suddenly became something to be ashamed of. No one ever mentioned it as "different', but now it was the glowing object on my face, like Rudolph's red nose, staring for everyone to see. I wanted to hide it away and fit in like all the other reindeer, but God made me different. It became problematic the older I got, as kids can sometimes be cruel. Tears would find a gentle caress as my mom stroked away the salty wetness and planted kisses all over my special eye. "This is your kiss from God", she would say. "So that every time you look in the mirror, you would see Him looking back at you". Like Jesus, she was my comfort in the storm. That's what parents do. We help our children face their differences with tenderness, courage, and confidence. Their difference is their "kiss from God.". By giving them the tools in childhood, we are preparing them to maneuver the pitfalls of adulthood. I wrote this simple story to help children embrace their differences as God's gift. Made in the image of the Father, we are each *"fearfully and wonderfully made."*. May God use it, and use you, to instill a godly confidence of self - acceptance in the heart of your child.

BJ FOSTER

Dedicated to my mom, who kissed away my tears.

God, God, when you look at me,
Tell me, tell me
What do you see?

Because I see a girl all chocolate
and round With hair that is
puffy and teeth like a clown

God sees a girl with the air of a queen
With dazzling wonder made to be seen
Sassy and bright for all to see
Like the humming buzz of a bumble bee.

God, God, when you look at me,
Tell me, tell me
What do you see?

Because I see a girl helpless and small
Stuck in leg braces barely walking at all.

God sees a girl on feet with wings
Leaping and flying
over everything. Running with
fireflies, Stomping on leaves Floating
on air, like the wind in the trees.

God, God, when you look at me,
Tell me, Tell me,
What do you see?

Because here I sit day after day,
With nothing but my mind to take me away

God sees a boy flying high in the sky
With the birds of the air and an eagle's eye.
Seeing the world in colorful rays
Roaming, only where the angel plays.

God, God, when you look at me,
Tell me, Tell me
What do you see?

Because I see a kid lost without sight
A kid dying, to just go ride a bike.

God sees a girl with eyes so bright
Painting the beauty of his sky at night
Seeing what no one else on earth sees
Like the whOOShing sound of a gentle breeze.

God, God, when
you look at me,
Tell me, Tell me
What do you see?

Because I see a face
covered in scars
Where kids joke and tease
and say I'm from Mars.

God sees beauty that makes his heart skip
Like the twists and turns of a
rollercoaster dip. Shining light on a world so
sweet. Spreading joy to everyone you meet.

God, God, when you look at me,
Tell me, Tell me
What do you see?

Because I see a kid lost in a fog
Sitting on a swing like a bump on a log.

God sees a creator of crazy new things
Like pOtiOns that bubble and shOes that ring.
A mind that is free to search the deep
For riddles He's hidden and secrets he keeps.

God, God, when you look at me,
Tell me, Tell me
What do you see?

I'm just a little kid,
no one listens at all
Well maybe if I
break something or
stumble and fall.

Little kids are what He want others to be
Trusting and caring with hearts full of glee.
Willing to go wherever he leads.
Sprinkling hOpe and planting his seeds.

Children, Children, when you look up high,
Tell me, Tell me
How do you see God in the sky?

I see a fountain spraying
water high in the air.
With joy and laughter
and lots of wet hair.

I see a builder of things
small and tall,
With his head thrown
back and having a ball.

16

I see the leader of a crazy air band, With guitars and cymbals and thousands of fans.

I see a puppy in flowers galore. Running and playing, looking for more.

My children, my children,
You know what He sees?

19

All of your beautiful faces,
Perfectly made, as He pleased.

Printed in the United States
by Baker & Taylor Publisher Services